For GW

The Christmas Eve Mouse
By Alice Mooney

THE CHRISTMAS EVE
MOUSE

Alice Mooney

It was a frosty and magical Christmas Eve on Bainbridge Island.

Snowflakes were twirling round me as I ventured out in search of a Christmas tree. Bainbridge Gardens was glistening with beautiful golden angels, jolly Santa decorations, twinkling lights and tinsel. On the counter, stood a little tree made of sparkling silver tinsel and glowing colored lights. The Christmas tree was so different and so beautiful, I knew right away that it was for me.

I was filled with joy, as I carried
the little silver tree out to my car.

I placed the little silver Christmas tree in the back of my car and drove through town on Winslow Way. The Shops were decorated in twinkling lights and strands of fresh garland.

A quick stop at Town & Country Market to pick up my favorite turkey, gravy and stuffing, for a special Christmas Eve dinner.

While driving home, I noticed a beautiful Christmas Star shining in the sky. A reminder that the true meaning of Christmas is love. A celebration of baby Jesus' birth. Then I said a prayer of thanks, as I drove home on the holy night.

At home, it was cozy sitting by the fireplace. The phone rang with merry wishes from family and friends. It was my first Christmas celebrating at home without them.

Later in the evening, after Christmas dinner, I went to the kitchen for a candy cane. The little silver tree was sparkling on the kitchen island. As I walked towards the counter, I started to recite a Christmas poem.

"Twas the night before Christmas, when all through the house, Not a creature was stirring, not even .....

...A MOUSE!

AAAAHHHHHHH!!!

I looked down and yelled "A MOUSE!"

As I ran down the hall to the bedroom, I looked back and saw the mouse following me! I yelled for help! The mouse was running right behind me all the way to the bedroom.

I jumped on the bed and picked up my cell phone. I contacted my friend GW, who said the mouse was more afraid of me, than I was of it. He said to make a loud noise and it will go away. So, I yelled again and the mouse slowly walked closer and closer towards me. He looked up at me on the bed. I yelled for help again and the mouse just stood there looking up at me. He was a different mouse, as he wasn't at all afraid of me. AAAHHHHH!!

So, I called my friends that live on the island. I asked Mr. T for help. He said "Alice calm down, I am on my way." and stayed on the phone as he drove over to help me.

As I stood on my bed waiting for help to arrive, the mouse started walking past my drawing table, over to the chair at my desk. He climbed up the leg of the chair. Then, the little mouse turned around and stared at me, as he sat atop of the chair. He sat and stared, as I cried and yelled for help.

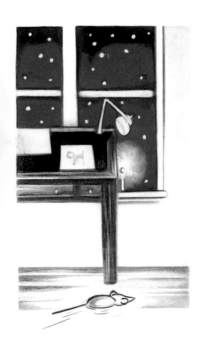

Mr. T arrived and walked up to the mouse and said "Oh this little guy? Alice, he likes you. He just wants to be your friend. He likes it here with you."

"What?" I said "My friend?? No, I don't think so." Then Mr. T said "Ok" and he picked up the little mouse and said "I will put him outside."

Mr. T dropped the little mouse outside the front door into the cold on Christmas Eve. I felt safe again and thanked Mr. T for his help as he went on his way.

I sat by the fireplace and wondered about the little mouse. What a strange thing to have happen on Christmas Eve. A visit from a little mouse.

I wondered for a moment, did the little mouse really want to be my friend? Did he like it here with me? It is cozy here and he seemed comfortable sitting on the chair. Then I wondered if the mouse was ok out in the cold by himself on Christmas Eve. So, I said a prayer for angels to protect and guide The Christmas Eve Mouse.

As I sat by the cozy fireplace, I started to get sleepy. I wondered as I dozed off, how The Christmas Eve Mouse spent his Christmas Eve out in the cold on Bainbridge Island ....

The wind was blowing snowflakes, as The Christmas Eve Mouse walked along the snowy trails of the island. He came across a Christmas present with a big green bow, sitting under a twinkling tree in the woods. He opened the box. Inside was a little red woolen Santa hat and jacket. A perfect size and fit to keep the little mouse warm.

The Christmas Eve Mouse was so happy with his new warm Christmas hat and jacket. It was a special gift left under the tree by Santa, who somehow knew The Christmas Eve Mouse would find it and need it.

The mouse was cozy in his new clothes as he kept walking along in the snow towards the harbor.

Up ahead near the harbor, was a beautiful Christmas Eve party. The Bainbridge Island bunnies were celebrating by candlelight, with Christmas dinner and candies.

The Christmas Eve Mouse didn't want to intrude on their party, so he said "Merry Christmas" to the bunnies and kept walking towards the harbor.

At the harbor, a horn blast out as the Bainbridge Island Ferry was leaving the dock and heading to Seattle.

The little mouse was getting tired and didn't know where to go.

When suddenly, The Christmas Eve Mouse heard loud Christmas music ringing out from a distance.

Jingle Bells!! Jingle Bells!! The Christmas Eve Mouse looked up and saw the Bainbridge Island, Holiday Music Fire Truck headed his way! The truck is an island tradition at Christmas, with bright lights glowing and Christmas music ringing out.

The firemen called out "Merry Christmas!" They asked the mouse if he needed help. "Yes, I am not sure where to go." said the little mouse. The firemen knew exactly who could help the mouse and said "Hop on the back for a ride on the Holiday Music Fire Truck." They drove the little mouse to find Santa, who was on the island filling stockings.

The Christmas Eve Mouse had fun riding on the fire truck and said thank you to the kind firemen. They found Santa just in time, at his last chimney stop on the island.

"HO HO HO!!" Santa said, with a big smile. "I was waiting for you little mouse. I need your help tonight and back at my castle at the North Pole. Would you like to be my helper?" The Christmas Eve Mouse smiled and said "Yes! Yes Santa, I would love to be your helper!"

The Christmas Eve Mouse and Santa said goodbye to Bainbridge Island. "Up, Up and Away!" Up to the twinkling stars in the sky, they flew in Santa's sleigh.

MERRY CHRISTMAS TO ALL

 TO ALL A GOOD NIGHT !

ALICE MOONEY IS AN AMERICAN
ILLUSTRATOR. HER WORK IS PUBLISHED
IN NATIONAL MAGAZINES AND
NEWSPAPERS SINCE 1991.

BORN IN BOSTON AND RAISED IN
HINGHAM MASSACHUSETTS, ALICE ALSO
LIVED IN A CANYON IN MALIBU BEFORE
MOVING TO BAINBRIDGE ISLAND IN 1996,
WHERE SHE CURRENTLY RESIDES.

ALICE MOONEY'S, THE CHRISTMAS EVE
MOUSE, IS BASED ON A TRUE STORY AND
IS ALICE'S FIRST CHILDREN'S BOOK.

SEE MORE AT ALICEMOONEY.COM

CPSIA information can be obtained
at www.ICGtesting.com
Printed in the USA
BVRC092105171221
624418BV00004B/57

* 9 7 8 1 0 0 6 2 3 3 8 0 7 *